The Postman

Gordon Winch & Gregory Blaxell
Illustrated by Jean Mulligan

Patch does not like cats.

Patch does not like cars.

Patch does not like birds.

Patch does not like bikes.

Patch does not like baths.

Patch does not like storms.

Patch does not like the
postman.